TOOTH AI

SHORT STORIES

In each of the following stories there is a wild or a dangerous animal. The animals can hurt and kill. And yet all the stories take place in houses, gardens, a small wood – safe, civilized places where we do not expect to meet wild and dangerous animals. So why are they there? Why has Saki brought these fierce creatures into our homes?

The answer is that we want them to be there. Of course, we do not want wolves in our gardens all the time; that would be very inconvenient. But sometimes – when we have an unwelcome visitor, or when we have to be polite when we want to be rude – sometimes a real wolf would be very useful indeed. Saki's animals are sometimes funny, and they are sometimes cruel. But they always bite through what we pretend, and uncover the real emotions beneath.

SAKI

Tooth and Claw

SHORT STORIES

Retold by
Rosemary Border

OXFORD UNIVERSITY PRESS

OXFORD BOOKWORMS LIBRARY
Human Interest

Tooth and Claw

SHORT STORIES

Stage 3 (1000 headwords)

Series Editor: Jennifer Bassett
Founder Editor: Tricia Hedge
Activities Editors: Jennifer Bassett and Alison Baxter

OXFORD
UNIVERSITY PRESS

Great Clarendon Street, Oxford OX2 6DP

Oxford University Press is a department of the University of Oxford.
It furthers the University's objective of excellence in research, scholarship,
and education by publishing worldwide in

Oxford New York

Auckland Cape Town Dar es Salaam Hong Kong Karachi
Kuala Lumpur Madrid Melbourne Mexico City Nairobi
New Delhi Shanghai Taipei Toronto

With offices in

Argentina Austria Brazil Chile Czech Republic France Greece
Guatemala Hungary Italy Japan Poland Portugal Singapore
South Korea Switzerland Thailand Turkey Ukraine Vietnam

OXFORD and OXFORD ENGLISH are registered trade marks of
Oxford University Press in the UK and in certain other countries

ISBN 978 0 19 479135 9

Printed in Hong Kong

ACKNOWLEDGEMENTS
Illustrated by: Jenny Brackley

Word count (main text): 8255 words

For more information on the Oxford Bookworms Library,
visit www.oup.com/bookworms

CONTENTS

Sredni Vashtar

C onradin was ten years old and was often ill.
    'The boy is not strong,' said the doctor. 'He will not live
much longer.' But the doctor did not know about Conradin's
imagination. In Conradin's lonely, loveless world, his
imagination was the only thing that kept him alive.

Conradin's parents were dead and he lived with his aunt.
The aunt did not like Conradin and was often unkind to him.
Conradin hated her with all his heart, but he obeyed her
quietly and took his medicine without arguing. Mostly he
kept out of her way. She had no place in his world. His real,
everyday life in his aunt's colourless, comfortless house was
narrow and uninteresting. But inside his small, dark head
exciting and violent thoughts ran wild. In the bright world
of his imagination Conradin was strong and brave. It was a
wonderful world, and the aunt was locked out of it.

The garden was no fun. There was nothing interesting to
do. He was forbidden to pick the flowers. He was forbidden
to eat the fruit. He was forbidden to play on the grass. But
behind some trees, in a forgotten corner of the garden, there
was an old shed.

Nobody used the shed, and Conradin took it for his own. To him it became something between a playroom and a church. He filled it with ghosts and animals from his imagination. But there were also two living things in the shed. In one corner lived an old, untidy-looking chicken. Conradin had no people to love, and this chicken was the boy's dearest friend. And in a dark, secret place at the back of the shed was a large wooden box with bars across the front. This was the home of a very large ferret with long, dangerous teeth and claws. Conradin had bought the ferret and its box from a friendly boy, who lived in the village. It had cost him all his money, but Conradin did not mind. He was most terribly afraid of the ferret, but he loved it with all his heart. It was his wonderful, terrible secret. He gave the ferret a strange and beautiful name and it became his god.

The aunt went to church every Sunday. She took Conradin with her, but to Conradin her church and her god were without meaning. They seemed grey and uninteresting. The true god lived in the shed, and his name was Sredni Vashtar.

Every Thursday, in the cool, silent darkness of the shed, Conradin took presents to his god. He took flowers in summer and fruits in autumn, and he made strange and wonderful songs for his god. Sometimes, on days when something important happened, Conradin took special presents. He stole salt from the kitchen and placed it carefully and lovingly in front of the ferret's box.

One day the aunt had the most terrible toothache. It continued for three days. Morning and evening Conradin

There were also two living things in the shed.

put salt in front of his god. In the end he almost believed that Sredni Vashtar himself had sent the toothache.

After a time the aunt noticed Conradin's visits to the shed.

'It's not good for him to play out there in the cold,' she said. She could always find a reason to stop Conradin enjoying himself. The next morning at breakfast she told Conradin that she had sold the chicken. She looked at Conradin's white face, and waited for him to cry or to be angry. But Conradin said nothing; there was nothing to say.

Perhaps the aunt felt sorry. That afternoon there was hot buttered toast for tea. Toast was usually forbidden. Conradin loved it, but the aunt said that it was bad for him. Also, it made extra work for the cook. Conradin looked at the toast and quietly took a piece of bread and butter.

'I thought you liked toast,' the aunt said crossly.

'Sometimes,' said Conradin.

In the shed that evening Conradin looked sadly at the empty corner where his chicken had lived. And, for the first time, he asked his ferret-god to do something for him.

'Do one thing for me, Sredni Vashtar,' he said softly.

He did not say what he wanted. Sredni Vashtar was a god, after all. There is no need to explain things to gods. Then, with a last look at the empty corner, Conradin returned to the world that he hated.

And every night, in the shed and in his bedroom, Conradin repeated again and again,

'Do one thing for me, Sredni Vashtar.'

So Conradin's visits to the shed continued. The aunt noticed, and went to look in the shed again.

'What are you keeping in that locked box?' she asked. 'I'm sure you're keeping an animal there. It's not good for you.'

Conradin said nothing.

The aunt searched his bedroom until she found the key to the box. She marched down to the shed. It was a cold afternoon, and Conradin was forbidden to go outside. From the window of the dining-room Conradin could just see the door of the shed. He stood and waited.

He saw the aunt open the shed door. She went inside. Now, thought Conradin, she has found the box. She is opening the door, and feeling about inside the box where my god lives.

'Do one thing for me, Sredni Vashtar,' said Conradin softly. But he said it without hope. She will win, he thought. She always wins. Soon she will come out of the shed and give her orders. Somebody will come and take my wonderful god away – not a god any more, just a brown ferret in a box. Then there will be nothing important in my life . . . The doctor will be right. I shall sicken and die. She will win. She always wins . . . In his pain and misery, Conradin began to sing the song of his god:

Sredni Vashtar went into battle.
His thoughts were red thoughts and his teeth were white.
His enemies called for peace but he brought them death.
Sredni Vashtar the Beautiful.

'What are you keeping in that locked box?' the aunt asked.

Suddenly he stopped singing and went nearer to the window. The door of the shed was still open. Slowly, very slowly the minutes went by. Conradin watched the birds on the grass. He counted them, always with one eye on that open door. The unsmiling housekeeper came in with the tea things. Still Conradin stood and watched and waited. Hope was growing, like a small, sick flower, in his heart. Very softly he sang his song again, and his hope grew and grew. And then he saw a very wonderful thing.

Out of the shed came a long, low, yellow-and-brown animal. There were red, wet stains around its mouth and neck.

'Sredni Vashtar!' said Conradin softly. The ferret-god made its way to the bottom of the garden. It stopped for a moment, then went quietly into the long grass and disappeared for ever.

'Tea is ready,' said the housekeeper. 'Where is your aunt?'

'She went down to the shed,' said Conradin.

And, while the housekeeper went down to call the aunt, Conradin took the toasting-fork out of the dining-room cupboard. He sat by the fire and toasted a piece of bread for himself. While he was toasting it and putting butter on it, Conradin listened to the noises beyond the dining-room door. First there were loud screams – that was the housekeeper. Then there was the cook's answering cry. Soon there came the sound of several pairs of feet. They were carrying something heavy into the house.

'Who is going to tell that poor child?' said the housekeeper.

Out of the shed came a long, low, yellow-and-brown animal.

'Well, someone will have to,' answered the cook. And, while they were arguing, Conradin made himself another piece of toast.

The Story-Teller

It was a hot, airless afternoon. The train was slow and the next stop was nearly an hour away. The people in the train were hot and tired. There were three small children and their aunt, and a tall man, who was a bachelor. The bachelor did not know the little family, and he did not want to know them.

The aunt and the children talked, but it was not a real conversation. It was more like a battle with a small housefly which will not go away. When the aunt spoke to the children, she always began with 'Don't . . .' When the children spoke to her, they always began with 'Why . . .' The bachelor said nothing aloud.

The small boy opened his mouth and closed it again. It made an interesting little noise, so he did it again. Open. Close. Open. Close.

'Don't do that, Cyril,' said the aunt. 'Come and look out of the window.' The boy closed his mouth and sat next to the window. He looked out at the green fields and trees.

'Why is that man taking those sheep out of that field?' he asked suddenly.

'Perhaps he's taking them to another field where there is more grass,' said the aunt. It was not a very good answer, and the boy knew it.

'But there is lots of grass in that field,' he said. 'The field is full of grass, Aunt. Why doesn't the man leave his sheep in that field?'

'I suppose the grass in the other field is better,' answered the aunt.

'Why is it better?' asked Cyril at once.

'Oh, look at those cows!' cried the aunt. There were cows in nearly all the fields along the railway line. Cyril did not look at the cows. He wanted an answer to his question.

'Why is the grass in the other field better?' he said again.

The bachelor gave them an angry look. The aunt saw him. He's a hard, unkind man, she thought. He doesn't like children. She searched for a suitable answer to Cyril's question, but could not find one.

The smaller girl began to say some words from a song:

'On the road to Mandalay, where the happy children play,' she began.

Then she stopped. She could not remember any more words, so she said the first words again, quietly but very clearly. Then she said them again. And again. And again.

The bachelor looked angrily at the girl, and then at the aunt.

'Come here and sit down quietly,' the aunt said quickly to the children. 'I'm going to tell you a story.'

The children moved slowly towards the aunt's seat. They

*Cyril did not look at the cows. He wanted an answer
to his question.*

already looked bored. Clearly, the aunt was not a famous story-teller.

The story was horribly uninteresting. It was about a little girl. She was not a beautiful child, but she was always very, very good. Everybody loved her because she was good. Finally, she fell into a lake and her friends saved her because she was so good, and they loved her so much.

'Did they only save her because she was good?' asked the bigger girl. 'Shouldn't we save bad people too, if they fall into a lake?' The bachelor wanted to ask the same question, but he said nothing.

'Well, yes, we should,' said the aunt. 'But I'm sure the little girl's friends ran specially fast because they loved her so much.'

'That was the stupidest story that I've ever heard,' said the bigger girl.

'I didn't listen after the first few words,' said Cyril, 'because it was so stupid.'

The smaller girl was already quietly repeating the words of her song for the twentieth time.

'You're not very successful as a story-teller,' the bachelor said suddenly from his corner.

The aunt looked at him in angry surprise. 'It's not easy to tell stories that children can understand,' she answered coldly.

'I don't agree with you,' said the bachelor.

'Perhaps *you* would like to tell them a story,' said the aunt. She gave him a cold little smile.

'Yes – tell us a story,' said the bigger girl.

'A long time ago,' began the bachelor, 'there was a little girl called Bertha, who was extraordinarily good. She always worked well at school. She always obeyed her teachers and her parents. She was never late, never dirty, and always ate all her vegetables. She was polite, she was tidy, and she never, never told lies.'

'Oh,' said the children. They were beginning to look bored already.

'Was she pretty?' asked the smaller girl.

'No,' said the bachelor. 'She wasn't pretty. But she was horribly good.'

'Horribly good. I like that!' said Cyril. The children began to look more interested. The words 'horrible' and 'good' together was a new idea for them, and it pleased them.

'Bertha was always good,' continued the bachelor. 'Because she was so good, Bertha had three medals. There was the "Never Late" medal. There was the "Politeness" medal. And there was the medal for the "Best Child in the World". They were very large medals. Bertha always wore them on her dress, and they clinked as she walked along. She was the only child in her town who had three medals. So everybody knew that she must be an extra good child.'

'Horribly good,' repeated Cyril happily.

'Everybody talked about Bertha's goodness. The king of that country heard about her, and he was very pleased. "Because Bertha is so good," he said, "she may come and walk in my palace gardens every Friday afternoon." The

14

BERTHA

*'Bertha wasn't pretty,' said the bachelor, 'but she
was horribly good.'*

king's gardens were famous. They were large and very beautiful, and children were usually forbidden to go in them.'

'Were there any sheep in the palace gardens?' asked Cyril.

'No,' said the bachelor, 'there were no sheep.'

'Why weren't there any sheep?' asked Cyril at once.

The aunt gave a little smile, and waited with interest for the bachelor's answer.

'There were no sheep in the king's gardens,' explained the bachelor, 'because the king's mother had once had a dream. In her dream a voice said to her, "Your son will be killed by a sheep, or by a clock falling on him." That is why the king never kept a sheep in his gardens or a clock in his palace.'

The aunt thought secretly that this was a very clever answer, but she stayed silent.

'Was the king killed by a sheep, or by a clock?' asked the bigger girl.

'He is still alive,' said the bachelor calmly, 'so we don't know if the dream was true or not. But, although there were no sheep, there were lots of little pigs running around everywhere.'

'What colour were the pigs?' asked the smaller girl.

'Black with white faces, white with black faces, all black, grey and white, and some were all white.'

The bachelor stopped for a moment, while the children's imaginations took in these wonderful pictures. Then he went on again,

'Bertha was sorry that there were no flowers in the palace

'There were lots of little pigs running around the palace gardens.'

gardens. She had promised her aunts that she would not pick any of the kind king's flowers. She wanted very much to be good and to keep her promise. So she was very cross when she found that there were no flowers to pick.'

'Why weren't there any flowers?'

'Because the pigs had eaten them all,' said the bachelor immediately. 'The gardeners had told the king that he couldn't have pigs *and* flowers, because pigs eat flowers. So the king decided to have pigs, and no flowers.'

The children thought that this was an excellent idea.

'Most people choose flowers,' said Cyril. He looked very pleased. 'But of course, pigs are *much* better than flowers.'

'There were lots of other wonderful things in the palace gardens,' the bachelor continued. 'There were lakes with gold and blue and green fish in them. There were trees with beautiful birds that could talk and say clever things. There were also birds that could sing popular songs.

'Well, on the first Friday afternoon in May, Bertha came to the king's gardens. The king's soldiers saw her beautiful white dress and her three medals for goodness, and they opened the doors to the gardens at once.

'Bertha walked up and down and enjoyed herself very much. As she walked along, the three medals on her beautiful white dress clinked against each other. She heard them clinking, and she thought: "I'm here in these lovely gardens because I am the Best Child in the World." She felt pleased and happy and very, very good.

'Just then a very big, hungry wolf came into the gardens.

It wanted to catch a fat little pig for its supper.'

'What colour was the wolf?' asked the children, who were listening to the story with great interest.

'He was grey,' said the bachelor, 'with a black tongue and angry yellow eyes. He had long black claws and big, strong, yellowish teeth. The wolf was hungry. He smelled the ground with his long grey nose. Then he saw Bertha's beautiful, clean white dress and began to move quietly towards her.

'Bertha saw the wolf and she wished she had not come to the gardens. "Oh, why did I come here?" she thought. "All the bad children are safe at home. I wish I wasn't an extraordinarily good child! Then I could be safe at home too." She ran as hard as she could, and the wolf came after her on his long grey legs.

'At last Bertha managed to reach some big, sweet-smelling myrtle bushes, and she hid herself in the thickest bush. The wolf walked round and round the bushes, with his angry yellow eyes and his long black tongue. But he couldn't see Bertha because the bushes were too thick, and he couldn't smell her because the smell of the myrtle was too strong. So after a while the wolf became bored, and decided to go and catch a little pig for his supper.

'Bertha was terribly frightened. Her heart beat very fast and her body shook with fear. Her arms shook and her legs shook. Her three medals for goodness shook too. And as they shook, they clinked together. The wolf was just moving away, when he heard the medals clinking, and he stopped to

19

'The wolf ate everything except Bertha's shoes, a few small pieces of
her dress, and the three medals for goodness.'

listen. The medals clinked again. The wolf's yellow eyes shone, and he ran into the myrtle bushes, pulled Bertha out, and ate her. He ate everything except her shoes, a few small pieces of her dress, and the three medals for goodness.'

'Were any of the little pigs killed?' asked Cyril.

'No, they all escaped.'

'The story began badly,' said the smaller girl, 'but it finished beautifully.'

'It is the most beautiful story that I have ever heard,' said the bigger girl.

'It is the *only* beautiful story I have ever heard,' said Cyril.

The aunt did not agree. 'It was a most improper story!' she said angrily. 'You mustn't tell children stories like that! You have destroyed years of careful teaching.'

'Well,' said the bachelor. He put on his coat and picked up his bags. 'The children sat still and were quiet for ten minutes while they listened to the story. And they didn't do that for *you*.'

'I feel sorry for that woman,' thought the bachelor as he stepped down from the train at the next station. 'What will people think when those children ask her for an improper story!'

Gabriel-Ernest

Cunningham had spent an agreeable week in the country with his friend Van Cheele. Now Van Cheele was driving his guest back to the station. Cunningham was unusually quiet on the journey, but Van Cheele talked all the time, so he did not notice his friend's silence.

Suddenly Cunningham spoke. 'There is a wild animal in your woods,' he said.

'A wild animal? A few rabbits, perhaps. Nothing very terrible, surely,' said Van Cheele. Cunningham said nothing.

'What did you mean about a wild animal?' asked Van Cheele later, at the station.

'Nothing. It was my imagination. Here is the train,' said Cunningham.

That afternoon Van Cheele went for a walk through his woods. He knew a little about plants and animals, and he enjoyed walking through the woods around his house and looking at the birds and flowers there. He also enjoyed telling everyone about them afterwards. Of course, he never saw anything very surprising – until that afternoon.

During his walk Van Cheele came to a deep pool under

some tall trees. He knew it well: after all, it was his pool. But today, he saw a boy of about sixteen lying on a large rock beside the pool. The boy was drying his wet, naked brown body in the sun. His hair was wet too, and he had long, golden, wolfish eyes. He turned those eyes towards Van Cheele with a look of lazy watchfulness.

Van Cheele was surprised to see the boy. Where does this wild-looking boy come from? he thought. Can he be the miller's son? He disappeared two months ago. People say he fell into the river. It's a fast-running river, and nobody ever found his body. I wonder? But the miller's boy was only a young child . . .

'What are you doing here?' asked Van Cheele.

'Enjoying the sunshine, of course,' said the boy.

'Where do you live?'

'Here, in these woods.'

'You can't live in these woods,' said Van Cheele.

'They are very nice woods,' said the boy politely.

'But where do you sleep at night?'

'I don't sleep at night. That's my busiest time.'

Van Cheele began to feel cross. What did the boy mean?

'What do you eat?' he asked.

'Meat,' said the boy. He opened his mouth, showing very white teeth.

'Meat? What kind of meat?'

'Well, if you must know, I eat rabbits, wild birds, chickens from the farm and young sheep from the hills. I like children when I can find them. But they're usually too well locked in

23

'I don't sleep at night. That's my busiest time,' said the boy.

at night. It's two months since I tasted child meat.'

The boy is joking about the children, thought Van Cheele. But perhaps he really is stealing animals from the woods and farms. I must find out more about this.

Aloud he said, 'You catch rabbits? You must be joking. Our rabbits are much too fast for you.'

'At night I hunt on four feet,' was the boy's surprising reply.

'You mean that you hunt with a dog?' guessed Van Cheele.

The boy sat up suddenly and laughed a strange, low laugh. To Van Cheele that laugh sounded horribly like a growl.

'I don't think any dog would like to hunt with me,' the boy said. 'Not at night . . .'

There is something horrible about this boy, thought Van Cheele. I don't like the way he looks and I don't like the way he talks.

'I can't let you stay in my woods,' he said aloud.

'Very well then – shall I come and live in your house?' replied the boy.

Van Cheele thought about his quiet, tidy house. No, he did not want this strange, wild boy at all. Of course, the boy was joking . . . but Van Cheele was not amused.

'If you don't go away,' he said, 'I shall have to call the police.'

At once the boy turned and jumped head-first into the pool. A moment later, his shining, wet body landed half-way up the grassy bank where Van Cheele was standing. Van Cheele stepped backwards. His foot slipped on the wet grass and he fell. He found himself lying on the grass with those wolfish yellow eyes uncomfortably near to his. He felt a moment of horrible fear. The boy laughed again, a laugh that was like the growl of a wild animal, then disappeared among the bushes.

'What an extraordinarily wild animal!' said Van Cheele as he picked himself up. And then he remembered Cunningham's words about a wild animal in his woods.

As he walked slowly home, Van Cheele thought about several things which had happened in and around the village recently. Perhaps this boy knows something about them, he thought . . . Something has been killing rabbits and birds in the woods lately. Something has been stealing the farmers' chickens and carrying off the young sheep from the hills. Is it possible that this wild boy is hunting at night with a fast, intelligent dog? The boy talked of hunting on four feet at night . . . But he also said that dogs did not like to hunt with him at night . . . Very strange indeed.

As Van Cheele walked along, he turned the questions over and over in his head. Suddenly he stopped. The miller's son! he said to himself. The child disappeared two months ago. Everyone thought that he had fallen into the river and been carried away. But the child's mother did not believe this. She said she had heard a scream – and the scream came from the hill, a long way away from the water.

It's impossible, of course, said Van Cheele to himself. But the child disappeared two months ago, and the boy talked about child meat. He was joking, of course . . . but what a horrible joke!

Van Cheele usually talked to his aunt about the birds, plants and animals he saw on his walks. But today he said nothing. He was an important man in his village. If there was a thief living in his woods, he did not want anyone to know. If people hear about the boy, he thought, perhaps they will want me to pay for their lost chickens and their disappearing sheep.

He was unusually quiet at dinner. 'What's the matter with you?' joked his aunt. 'Did you see a wolf on your walk?'

At breakfast the next morning Van Cheele realized that he still felt uncomfortable about yesterday's adventure. I know what I'll do, he said to himself. I'll take the train to London and I'll go and see Cunningham. I'll ask him if he was joking when he said there was a wild animal in my woods.

After he had decided this, Van Cheele felt better. He sang a happy little song as he walked to the sitting-room for his morning cigarette. His fat old dog walked beside him.

As Van Cheele entered the sitting-room, the song died on his lips and his dog ran away with his tail between his legs. There on the day-bed, with his hands comfortably behind his head, lay the boy from the woods. He was drier than yesterday, but he was still naked.

'What are you doing here?' asked Van Cheele angrily.

'You told me I couldn't stay in the woods,' said the boy calmly.

'But I didn't tell you to come here. What if my aunt sees you? What will she think?'

Van Cheele was unusually quiet at dinner.

Van Cheele hurriedly covered his unwanted guest's nakedness with a newspaper. At that moment his aunt entered the room.

'This is a poor boy,' explained Van Cheele quickly. 'He has lost his way – and lost his memory too. He doesn't know who he is, or where he comes from.'

Miss Van Cheele was very interested. 'Perhaps his name is on his underclothes,' she said.

'He has lost his underclothes too,' said Van Cheele. The newspaper was slipping off the boy's naked body. Van Cheele hurried to replace it.

Miss Van Cheele was a kind old lady. She felt sorry for this naked, helpless child.

'We must help him,' she said. She sent the housekeeper to a neighbour's house to borrow some clothes.

Soon the boy was clean and tidy, and dressed in shirt, trousers and shoes. Van Cheele thought he looked just as strange and wolfish as before. But Miss Van Cheele thought he was sweet.

'We must give him a name until we know who he really is,' she said. 'Gabriel-Ernest, I think. Those are nice, suitable names.'

Van Cheele agreed. But he was not sure that the boy was a nice, suitable boy. Van Cheele's old dog, when he saw the boy, had run away in fear and would not come back into the house. Van Cheele decided to go and see Cunningham at once.

As he got ready to go to the station, his aunt was busily

Miss Van Cheele was very interested. 'Perhaps the boy's name is on his underclothes,' she said.

arranging a children's tea party in the church hall.

'Gabriel-Ernest will help me with the little ones,' she said happily.

When Van Cheele got to London, Cunningham did not want to talk at first. 'You'll think I'm crazy,' he said.

'But what did you see?' asked Van Cheele.

'I saw something – something unbelievable. On the last evening of my visit to you I was standing half-hidden in the bushes, watching the sun go down. Suddenly I noticed a naked boy. He has been swimming in a pool somewhere, I said to myself. He was standing on the hillside and he too was watching the sun go down. Then the sun disappeared behind the hill and its light was gone. At the same moment a very surprising thing happened – the boy disappeared too.'

'What? He disappeared just like that?' said Van Cheele excitedly.

'No. It was much more horrible than that. On the open hillside where the boy had been, I saw a large, blackish-grey wolf with long white teeth and yellow eyes. You'll think I'm crazy—'

But Van Cheele did not wait. He was running towards the station as fast as he could. He did not know what he could do. I can't send my aunt a message, he thought. What can I say? 'Gabriel-Ernest is a werewolf'? My aunt will think I'm joking. I MUST get home before sundown.

He caught his train. With painful slowness it carried him to the station a few miles from his home. He took a taxi to his village.

'Take me to the church hall – and hurry!' he ordered. The taxi drove along the quiet country roads, and the sky turned pink and purple as the sun got lower and lower in the west.

His aunt was putting away some uneaten cakes and sandwiches when he arrived.

'Where is Gabriel-Ernest?' screamed Van Cheele.

'He's taking little Jack Toop home,' said his aunt calmly. 'It was getting so late. I didn't want to send the dear little boy home alone. Isn't the sky beautiful this evening?'

But Van Cheele had no time to talk about the beautiful sky. He ran like the wind down the narrow road that went to the Toops' house. On one side was the fast-running river, on the other was the dark hillside. In a minute I'll catch up with them, Van Cheele thought.

Then the sun went down behind the hill and the whole world became grey and cold. Van Cheele heard a short scream of fear, and he knew he was too late.

Nobody ever saw little Jack Toop or Gabriel-Ernest again. Gabriel-Ernest's clothes were found lying in the road.

'Poor little Jack fell into the river,' said Miss Van Cheele. 'And dear Gabriel-Ernest took off his clothes and jumped into the river to try to save him.'

Mrs Toop had eleven other children and did not cry too long for her lost son. But Miss Van Cheele was terribly sad about Gabriel-Ernest.

'He must have a memorial in the church,' she said. She chose the words herself:

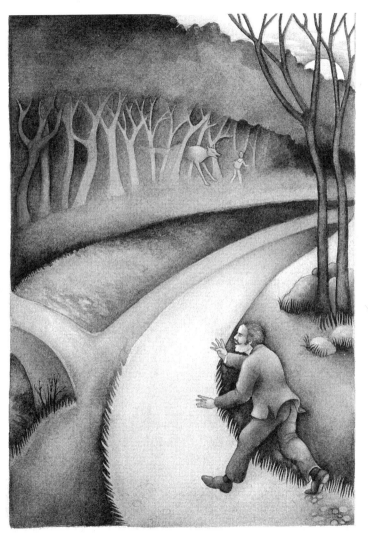

Van Cheele ran like the wind down the narrow road that went to the Toops' house.

GABRIEL-ERNEST,
AN UNKNOWN BOY
WHO BRAVELY GAVE HIS LIFE
FOR ANOTHER.

Van Cheele usually did what his aunt wanted. But he refused to give any money at all for Gabriel-Ernest's memorial.

Tobermory

It was a cold, rain-washed afternoon in late August. Lady Blemley and her guests were sitting round the tea table. Everyone was listening open-mouthed to Mr Cornelius Appin.

Although he was one of her guests, Lady Blemley did not know Mr Appin well. She had invited him to stay at Blemley House because she had heard that he was clever. But until teatime that day he had not done or said anything clever. He did not play tennis, or sing, or make intelligent conversation. But now Mr Appin was describing a most extraordinary discovery and the other guests were listening with deep interest.

'Are you telling us that you have found a way of teaching animals to talk?' Sir Wilfrid was saying. 'And our dear old Tobermory is your first successful student?'

'I have studied this problem for seventeen years,' said Mr Appin, 'but I didn't have any real success until eight or nine months ago. Of course, I have studied thousands of animals, but recently I have worked only with cats. A cat, of course, is a wild animal who agrees to live with you. All cats are intelligent, but naturally some cats are more intelligent than others. When I met Tobermory a week ago, I realized at once that here was an extraordinarily intelligent cat, a very special cat indeed. In Tobermory, I found the student I needed. With him I have succeeded in my plan.'

Nobody laughed, and nobody actually said 'Rubbish', although Clovis's lips moved silently . . .

'And have you really taught Tobermory,' asked Miss Resker, 'to say and understand short, easy words?'

'My dear Miss Resker,' said Mr Appin patiently, 'we teach little children and very slow, stupid adults in that way. But Tobermory is a most intelligent cat. He can speak English as well as you or I can.'

This time Clovis said 'Rubbish!' aloud.

Sir Wilfrid was more polite, but it was clear that he did not believe Mr Appin's story.

'Shall we bring the cat in here and hear him for ourselves?' said Lady Blemley.

Sir Wilfrid went off to look for Tobermory.

'Mr Appin will try to be clever,' said Miss Resker happily, 'but if we watch him carefully, we shall see his lips move.'

In a minute Sir Wilfrid returned, looking very excited.

'It's true, you know!' he said. 'I found Tobermory sleeping in the smoking-room, and called out to him to come for his tea. He lifted his head and opened one eye. I said, "Come on, Toby, don't keep us waiting!" and he said calmly, "I'll come when I'm ready!" I couldn't believe my ears!'

The guests all started talking at once, while Mr Appin sat

silently and looked very pleased with himself indeed.

Then Tobermory entered the room and calmly walked over to the tea table. The conversation stopped. Nobody knew what to say to a talking cat. At last Lady Blemley spoke:

'Would you like some milk, Tobermory?' she asked in a high, unnatural voice.

'I don't mind if I do,' answered Tobermory. Lady Blemley's hand shook with excitement and some of the milk went onto the carpet.

'Oh dear! I'm so sorry,' she said.

'I don't mind. It isn't my carpet, after all,' replied Tobermory.

There was another silence, then Miss Resker asked politely, 'Did you find it difficult to learn English, Tobermory?'

Tobermory looked straight through her with his bright green eyes. Clearly, he did not answer questions that did not interest him.

'What do you think of the intelligence of people?' asked Mavis Pellington.

'Which people's intelligence?' asked Tobermory coldly.

'Well, my intelligence, for example,' said Mavis with a little laugh.

'You make things very uncomfortable for me,' said Tobermory, although he did not look at all uncomfortable. 'When Lady Blemley wanted to invite you here, Sir Wilfrid was not pleased. "Mavis Pellington is the stupidest woman I know," he said. "That's why I want to invite her," Lady

'I don't mind. It isn't my carpet, after all,' replied Tobermory.

Blemley replied. "I want her to buy my old car, and she's stupid enough to do that." '

'It isn't true!' cried Lady Blemley. 'Don't believe him, Mavis!'

'If it isn't true,' said Mavis coldly, 'why did you say this morning that your car would be just right for me?'

Major Barfield did his best to help. He tried to start a new conversation. 'How are you getting on with your little black and white lady friend in the garden?' he asked Tobermory.

Everybody realized at once that this was a mistake.

Tobermory gave him an icy look. 'We do not usually discuss these things in polite company,' he said. 'But I have watched you a little since you have been in this house. I think perhaps you would not like me to discuss *your* lady friends.'

The Major's face became very red, and all the other guests began to look worried and uncomfortable. What was Tobermory going to say next?

'Would you like to go down to the kitchen now, Tobermory,' asked Lady Blemley politely, 'and see if the cook has got your dinner ready?'

'No, thank you,' said Tobermory. 'I've only just had my tea. I don't want to make myself sick.'

'Cats have nine lives, you know,' said Sir Wilfrid with a laugh.

'Possibly,' answered Tobermory. 'But only one stomach.'

'Lady Blemley!' cried Mrs Cornett, 'don't send that cat to the kitchen. He will talk about us to the cook!'

Everyone was very worried now. They remembered

uncomfortably that Tobermory moved freely all over the house and gardens, at all hours of the day and night. He could look into any of the bedrooms if he wanted to. What had he seen? What had he heard? Nobody's secrets were safe now.

'Oh, why did I come here?' cried Agnes Resker, who could never stay silent for long.

'You know very well why you came here,' said Tobermory immediately. 'You came for the food, of course. I heard you talking to Mrs Cornett in the garden. You said that the Blemleys were terribly boring people, but they had an excellent cook.'

'You mustn't believe him!' cried Agnes. 'I never said that, did I, Mrs Cornett?'

'Later, Mrs Cornett repeated your words to Bertie van Tahn,' said Tobermory. 'She said, "That Resker woman will go anywhere for four good meals a day," and Bertie said—'

Just then Tobermory looked out of the window and saw the doctor's big yellow cat crossing the garden. Immediately he disappeared through the open window.

Everyone started talking at once, and Mr Appin found himself in a storm of angry questions.

'You must stop this at once,' everyone said to him. 'What will happen if Tobermory teaches other cats to talk? We shall never have a moment's peace!'

'It's possible that he has taught the gardener's cat,' replied Mr Appin thoughtfully, 'but I don't believe he has had time to teach any other cats.'

Just then Tobermory saw the doctor's big yellow cat crossing the garden.

'Then,' said Mrs Cornett, 'although Tobermory is a valuable cat, he and the gardener's cat must die. Don't you agree, Lady Blemley?'

'You're right,' said Lady Blemley sadly. 'My husband and I love Tobermory – well, we did before this afternoon – but now, of course, he must die as soon as possible.'

'We will poison his dinner,' said Sir Wilfrid, 'and I will kill the gardener's cat myself. The gardener won't like it, but I'll say it has some kind of disease—'

'But what about my discovery?' cried Mr Appin. 'What about all my years of work? Are you going to destroy my only successful student?'

'You can go and teach the cows on the farm,' said Mrs Cornett coldly, 'or the elephants at the zoo. Elephants are very intelligent, they tell me, and elephants don't hide behind chairs or under beds and listen to people's conversations.'

Mr Appin knew when he was beaten.

Dinner that evening was not a success. Sir Wilfrid had had a difficult time with the gardener's cat and later with the gardener. Agnes Resker refused to eat anything, while Mavis Pellington ate her meal in silence. Everyone was waiting for Tobermory. A plate of poisoned fish stood ready for him in the dining-room, but he did not come home. Nobody talked much, and nobody laughed. It was a most uncomfortable meal.

After dinner the Blemleys and their guests sat in the smoking-room. Everyone was quiet and worried and nobody wanted to play cards. At eleven o'clock the cook and the housekeeper went to bed. They left the kitchen window open for Tobermory as usual, but he did not come.

At two o'clock Clovis spoke:

'He won't come home tonight. He's probably in the newspaper office selling them his story. They'll love it. The story will be the excitement of the year.'

After that everyone went to bed, but nobody slept.

In the morning Tobermory had still not come home. Breakfast was another quiet, uncomfortable meal. Then, half-way through the coffee, the gardener brought in Tobermory's blood-stained body.

'Look at his claws!' cried Clovis. 'He's been fighting!' And there, on Tobermory's claws, was the yellow hair of the doctor's cat.

By lunchtime most of the guests had left Blemley House. Lady Blemley began to feel better. She took out her pen and paper and wrote a very angry letter to the doctor about the death of her valuable cat.

Tobermory was Mr Appin's only successful student. A few weeks after Tobermory's death an elephant escaped from the Dresden Zoo and killed an English visitor.

The zoo keeper said that the elephant had always been a calm and gentle animal before. But suddenly it seemed to become very angry with the English visitor, who was talking to it.

The dead man's name was reported in the newspapers as Oppin, but his first name was Cornelius.

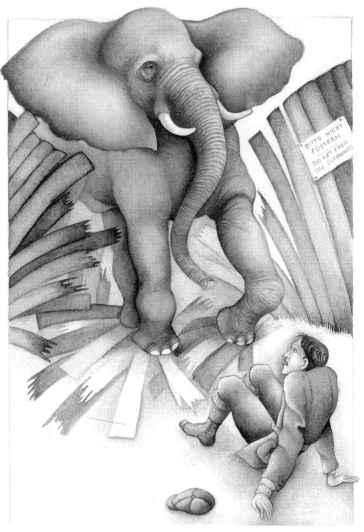

*Suddenly the elephant seemed to become very angry
with the English visitor.*

'If Appin was trying to teach the poor elephant to speak German,' said Clovis, 'I'm not surprised it killed him.'

The She-Wolf

To Leonard Bilsiter the real world was not very agreeable or interesting. He preferred to live in an 'unseen world' of his imagination. Children are often very good at this, but they are happy in their own dream worlds and do not try to make other people believe them. Leonard Bilsiter talked about 'the unseen world' to anyone who would listen to him.

Nothing very strange happened to Leonard, until one year he travelled by train across Eastern Europe. He had a long conversation with a Russian passenger, who talked about magic and 'hidden powers' in a most interesting way. Leonard listened excitedly. He came home with many stories about the strange, dark mysteries which he called Siberian Magic.

His aunt, Cecilia Hoops, was deeply interested in Leonard's Siberian Magic. When she told her friends about it ('My dears, he took a garden vegetable and changed it into a bird in front of my eyes!'), her friends realized that she also had a wonderful imagination.

Leonard, together with his hidden powers, was invited to Mary Hampton's house-party. Several other people were also staying in the house, and they all had to listen to Leonard talking about the mysteries of the unseen world.

'Do please change me into a wolf, Mr Bilsiter,' said Mrs Hampton during lunch on the day of his arrival.

'My dear Mary,' said her husband. 'What a strange idea!'

'A she-wolf, of course,' continued Mrs Hampton. 'I don't want to change into a man as well as an animal!'

'We should not joke about the unseen world,' said Leonard.

'Oh, I'm not joking, I promise you. But don't change me into a wolf tonight. I want to play cards, and there are only eight of us in the house today. I've invited some more people to come here tomorrow. Wait until tomorrow night.'

Leonard was not amused. 'Mrs Hampton, you really must not laugh at these dark mysteries. They can be stronger and more dangerous than we realize.'

Clovis Sangrail listened silently to this conversation, and after lunch he spoke to Lord Pabham in the smoking-room.

'Tell me, Lord Pabham,' began Clovis. 'Have you got a she-wolf in your zoo at Pabham Park? A quiet, friendly she-wolf?'

'There's Louisa,' said Lord Pabham thoughtfully. 'She's very quiet and gentle. Why do you ask?'

'I'd like to borrow her tomorrow evening,' said Clovis lightly. 'May I, please?'

'Tomorrow night?' repeated Lord Pabham in surprise.

'Yes. Wolves usually sleep during the day, don't they? So a night-time journey won't hurt her. Could you ask one of

Clovis Sangrail listened silently to this conversation.

your men to bring Louisa here when it is dark? Then he can take her quietly into the conservatory at the same time as Mrs Hampton leaves the dining-room.'

Lord Pabham looked at Clovis in surprise. Then he smiled. 'I understand!' he said. 'You're going to try a little Siberian Magic. And has Mrs Hampton agreed to help you?'

'Mary has promised – if your she-wolf is quiet and gentle.'

'Louisa won't give you any trouble,' said Lord Pabham.

The next day several more guests arrived. Leonard Bilsiter enjoyed telling them all about Siberian Magic and hidden powers. He talked all through dinner. When the coffee arrived at the end of the meal, Leonard's aunt spoke.

'Dear Leonard,' she said, 'please show us your powers. Change something into another shape.' She turned to the other guests. 'He can do it if he wants to,' she told them.

'Oh, please show us,' said Mavis Pellington excitedly.

'Well . . .' began Leonard. 'If somebody will give me a small coin . . .'

'Oh, surely you aren't going to do stupid things with disappearing coins?' said Clovis. 'We want to see something really surprising.'

'That's right,' said Mary Hampton. 'Why don't you change me into a wolf? You promised!' She got up from the table and walked into the conservatory with a bowl of fruit for her macaws.

'I have already warned you,' said Leonard seriously. 'It is dangerous to joke about these things.'

'I don't believe you can do it!' laughed Mary from the

conservatory. As she spoke, she disappeared behind a large green plant.

'Mrs Hampton—' began Leonard seriously. Then an icy wind seemed to fill the dining-room, and at the same time Mrs Hampton's macaws began to scream.

'What's wrong with those stupid birds, Mary?' asked her husband. Just then, a big grey wolf stepped out from behind the large green plant.

Leonard's aunt saw it first. 'Leonard!' she screamed. 'Bring Mrs Hampton back at once! We don't want a dangerous wild animal in here!'

'I – I don't know how to bring her back,' said Leonard in a small, frightened voice.

'Rubbish!' shouted Mr Hampton. 'You changed my dear wife into a wolf. Now you must bring her back again!'

'Please believe me,' said Leonard. '*I* didn't change your wife into a wolf.'

'Then where is she, and how did that animal get into the conservatory?' asked Mr Hampton angrily.

'Of course, we must believe you when you say that you didn't change Mrs Hampton into a wolf,' said Clovis politely. 'But you must agree that it all looks very strange.'

'How can you stand there arguing,' cried Mavis Pellington, 'with a wild animal in the house?'

'Lord Pabham,' began Mr Hampton, 'you know a lot about wild animals . . .'

'I *buy* all my animals,' said Lord Pabham. 'I have never found one in a conservatory before. But this is a wolf, I am

Just then, a big grey wolf stepped out from behind the large green plant.

sure of that. I think it's probably a North American she-wolf—'

'Oh, who cares where it came from!' screamed Mavis, as the wolf came a few steps further into the room. 'Can't you offer it some food, and take it away safely somewhere before it bites somebody?'

'If this animal is really Mrs Hampton,' said Clovis, 'she's just had an excellent dinner. She won't be interested in food.'

'Oh, Leonard,' cried his aunt, 'can't you use your wonderful powers to change this terrible animal into something small and gentle, like a rabbit?'

'I don't think Mr Hampton would like that,' said Clovis.

'You're right!' shouted Mr Hampton. 'I forbid it!'

'All my wolves love sugar,' said Lord Pabham. 'If you like, I'll offer this one a piece.' He took a piece of sugar from the table and pushed it along the floor towards Louisa. She ate it quickly and then, clearly hoping for more sugar, she followed Lord Pabham out of the room.

The guests left the table thankfully and hurried into the conservatory. It was empty. Mrs Hampton had disappeared.

'The door to the garden is locked on the inside!' said Clovis. (He had quickly turned the key while he was pretending to try the lock.)

Everyone turned towards Leonard Bilsiter.

'If you have not changed my wife into a wolf,' said Mr Hampton, 'will you please explain where she has gone? Clearly she could not go out through a locked door – so where is she?'

*The guests left the table thankfully and hurried
into the conservatory.*

'I tell you, I had nothing to do with it!' repeated Leonard again and again. But nobody believed him.

'I'm leaving,' said Mavis Pellington. 'I refuse to stay another hour in this house.'

Just then Mary Hampton entered the room.

'What happened?' she asked crossly. 'Someone has been playing a stupid game with me. I found myself in the kitchen, eating sugar from Lord Pabham's hand. I hate stupid games, and my doctor has forbidden me to eat sugar.'

'Well, my dear . . .' began Mr Hampton. Mrs Hampton listened excitedly as he explained.

'So you really did change me into a wolf, Mr Bilsiter?' cried Mrs Hampton.

'No, no,' said Leonard. 'It's all a mistake.'

'Actually, I did it,' said Clovis. 'You see, I spent two years in Russia, and I know a little about Siberian Magic. Of course, I don't like to talk about it. But when other people talk a lot of rubbish about hidden powers, I like to show what Siberian Magic can *really* do . . . May I please have a drink? I feel a little tired now.'

Leonard Bilsiter looked at Clovis with hate in his eyes. At that moment he wished strongly that he could change Clovis into some small helpless animal, and then step on him very hard.

GLOSSARY

aunt the sister of your father or mother

bachelor a man who is not married

bank the ground along the side of a river, lake or pool

bar a long piece of something hard (bars fixed to a box or cage stop animals from getting out)

believe to think that something is true

bush a plant like a short, thick tree, with many branches

claws the sharp nails on some animals' feet

clink *(v)* to make a noise like coins knocking together

conservatory a room with glass walls and roof, built on the side of a house

dining-room a room where people eat their meals

elephant a very big, grey animal with a very long nose

ferret a small but dangerous animal, used for catching rabbits

forbidden not allowed or permitted

god a spirit that people think has power over them and nature

growl *(v)* to make a low, angry noise in the throat, like a dog

guest a person who is invited to stay or eat in somebody's house

horrible making you very frightened or unhappy

hunt *(v)* to chase and catch wild animals for food

imagination making pictures in your head

improper rude or unsuitable; wrong for that situation

intelligence the ability to think, understand and reason

joke *(v)* to say things that are funny and amusing, or not serious

king the man who rules a country and who belongs to a royal family

lord a title for an important man

macaw a big noisy bird that can learn to talk

magic   strange powers that can make wonderful and unusual things happen

major   a title for an army officer

medal   a piece of metal, like a coin, given to people to show that they have done something special

memorial   a building, a stone, etc. with the name of a dead person, to help people remember him/her

memory   being able to remember things

miller   a man who works in a mill, a building where corn is made into flour

myrtle bush   a green plant with sweet-smelling white flowers

naked   not wearing any clothes

pig   a farm animal with a fat body and short legs

poison   something that will kill you or make you very ill if you eat or drink it

pool   a small lake

power   being able to do things

rabbit   a small animal with long ears, which lives in holes under the ground

shed   a small wooden building in a garden

slip *(v)*   to slide accidentally and almost fall over

stain   a dirty or coloured mark (e.g. of blood, coffee, etc.) on something

thought *(n)*   something that you think

toast *(n)*   bread that is cooked until it is hot and brown

werewolf   an imaginary animal that is a man in the day and a wolf at night

wolf   a wild animal like a big dog, which hunts and kills other animals

zoo   a place where wild animals are kept for people to look at

Tooth and Claw

SHORT STORIES

ACTIVITIES

Before Reading

1 **Read the back cover. How much do you know now about Conradin? For each sentence, circle Y (Yes) or N (No).**

   1 Conradin is a boy. Y/N
   2 Conradin lives with his mother and father. Y/N
   3 Conradin loves his aunt. Y/N
   4 Conradin keeps an animal in his bedroom. Y/N
   5 Conradin prays to the animal. Y/N

2 **Conradin asks the animal to do one thing for him. Can you guess what it is? Choose one of these answers.**

   1 to give him a lot of money
   2 to kill someone for him
   3 to find his mother and father
   4 to change his aunt into an animal

3 **Now read the story introduction on the first page of the book. Are these sentences true (T) or false (F)?**

   1 There is a wild animal in each of the stories.
   2 The stories happen in wild places.
   3 People never want wild animals in their homes.
   4 These stories will sometimes make you laugh.

While Reading

Read *Sredni Vashtar* up to page 5, and answer these questions.

1 What kept Conradin alive?
2 Why did Conradin hate his aunt?
3 Where did Conradin play?
4 Who was Conradin's best friend?
5 What kind of animal did Conradin keep in the box in the shed?
6 How did Conradin feel about the animal in the box?
7 What did Conradin's aunt do with the chicken?
8 Why didn't Conradin eat the toast?
9 What was the name of Conradin's god?
10 What did Conradin think that his aunt was going to do when she went to the shed for the second time?

Before you read the end of the story, can you guess what is going to happen? For each sentence, circle Y (Yes) or N (No).

1 Conradin's aunt will kill the ferret. Y/N
2 Conradin will die. Y/N
3 The ferret will kill Conradin's aunt. Y/N
4 The ferret will frighten Conradin's aunt and she will agree to let Conradin keep it. Y/N

Read *The Story-Teller*. Who said this, and to whom? Who or what were they talking about?

1 'Don't do that, Cyril.'
2 'Why is it better?'
3 'That was the stupidest story I've ever heard.'
4 'Was she pretty?'
5 'Bertha always wore them on her dress, and they clinked as she walked along.'
6 'He is still alive, so we don't know if the dream was true or not.'
7 'Black with white faces, white with black faces, all black . . .'
8 'He was grey, with a black tongue and angry yellow eyes.'
9 'Oh, why did I come here?'
10 'You have destroyed years of careful teaching.'
11 'And they didn't do that for you.'

Read *Gabriel-Ernest*. Are these sentences true (T) or false (F)? Rewrite the false ones with the correct information.

1 Van Cheele told Cunningham that there was a wild animal in the woods.
2 When Van Cheele first saw the boy, he was swimming in the pool.
3 People said that the miller's son fell into the river.
4 The boy said that he slept in the woods at night.
5 When the boy said that he ate children, Van Cheele thought that he was telling the truth.
6 The boy said that he hunted at night on four feet.
7 Van Cheele liked the boy.

8 When Van Cheele saw the boy in his sitting-room, the boy was wearing his underclothes.

9 Van Cheele's dog liked the boy but Miss Van Cheele was frightened of him.

10 Cunningham told Van Cheele that when the sun went down, the boy disappeared and a wolf appeared.

11 Miss Van Cheele asked Gabriel-Ernest to take Jack Toop home.

12 Miss Van Cheele thought that Gabriel-Ernest killed Jack Toop.

Read *Tobermory*. Choose the best question-word for these questions and then answer them.

How / What / Who / Why

1 . . . did Lady Blemley invite Mr Cornelius Appin to stay at her house?

2 . . . had Mr Appin studied for seventeen years?

3 . . . had Mr Appin taught Tobermory to do?

4 . . . did everyone stop talking when Tobermory came into the room?

5 . . . did Lady Blemley invite Mavis Pellington to stay?

6 . . . asked Tobermory about his lady friend?

7 . . . was everyone very worried about Tobermory?

8 . . . came to stay with the Blemleys because they had a good cook?

9 . . . did Sir Wilfrid kill the gardener's cat?

10 . . . did Tobermory die?

11 . . . did Cornelius Appin die?

Read *The She-Wolf*. Match these halves of sentences and put them in the right order to make a summary of the story. Begin with number 3.

1 After dinner, Mary Hampton again asked Mr Bilsiter to change her into a she-wolf,

2 After Clovis Sangrail heard this,

3 After Leonard Bilsiter met a Russian on a train,

4 and told them that she had found herself in the kitchen eating sugar.

5 Mary Hampton asked him to change her into a she-wolf.

6 but Leonard said that he couldn't bring her back.

7 Leonard Bilsiter wanted to kill him.

8 and as she spoke, she disappeared behind a big plant.

9 When Clovis said that he had changed her into a wolf using Siberian Magic,

10 and found that the door was locked.

11 he asked to borrow a quiet she-wolf from Lord Pabham's zoo the next evening.

12 he talked about Siberian Magic all the time.

13 Then a cold wind seemed to fill the room

14 and she followed him out of the room, hoping for more sugar.

15 Just then, Mary Hampton came into the room

16 Leonard's aunt told him to bring Mrs Hampton back

17 So Lord Pabham gave the wolf a piece of sugar

18 and a big grey wolf appeared from behind the plant.

19 The guests hurried into the conservatory

20 So when Mr Bilsiter was staying with the Hamptons,

After Reading

1 Here is a newspaper report about Bertha's death. Fill in the gaps. Use one word in each gap.

A young girl called Bertha was killed yesterday while she was walking in the _____ gardens. She was extraordinarily _____ and always _____ her teachers and her parents. She was never dirty and she never _____ lies. She had three _____, which she always _____ on her dress: one because she was never _____, one because she was always _____, and one because she was the _____ Child in the World. The medals _____ as she walked along and everybody knew that she was extra good. When the _____ heard about her, he said that she could come and walk in his gardens every Friday _____. Children were usually _____ to walk in the gardens, which were very beautiful. There were lakes and trees and birds, but no _____, because the king had lots of little _____ running around everywhere. The king's _____ opened the gates for Bertha, but they never saw her again. They found her shoes, a few _____ of her dress, and her medals on the ground near some _____ bushes. They think that perhaps a _____ came to get a pig for its _____, but ate Bertha instead.

2 A policeman asked Miss Van Cheele some questions about Gabriel-Ernest. Put the conversation in the correct order and add the names. The policeman speaks first (number 13).

1 _____ 'And so Mr Van Cheele ran after them?'

2 _____ 'Did he tell you that his name was Gabriel-Ernest?'

3 _____ 'He was on his way back from London. He arrived just after the boys had left the church hall.'

4 _____ 'And what happened at the end of the party?'

5 _____ 'I'm not really sure. He just appeared one day in our sitting-room.'

6 _____ 'And where was Mr Van Cheele at that time?'

7 _____ 'He was naked? Didn't you think that was strange?'

8 _____ 'No, he'd lost his memory, so I gave him a name.'

9 _____ 'Didn't he have a name on his clothes?'

10 _____ 'Not at all. I thought he was a very nice boy. So I asked him to help me with the children's tea party.'

11 _____ 'I'm afraid he wasn't wearing any clothes.'

12 _____ 'Worried about what?'

13 _____ 'Who exactly was this Gabriel-Ernest?'

14 _____ 'Well, it was getting late, so I asked dear Gabriel-Ernest to take little Jack Toop home.'

15 _____ 'Worried about an accident, I think. And he was right. Poor little Jack fell into the river, and dear, brave Gabriel-Ernest jumped in after him.'

16 _____ 'Yes. He seemed very worried.'

The policeman then made some notes about questions to ask Van Cheele. Use these words to make four questions. Then write a fifth question of your own.

1 when / meet / Gabriel-Ernest?
2 why / go / London?
3 why / run / after the boys?
4 what / find / in the road?

3 Tobermory made people very uncomfortable. Here are some of the things that he said and did. Complete the sentences in your own words.

1 When Sir Wilfrid called him to tea, he _____.
2 When Miss Resker asked if it was difficult to learn English, he _____.
3 He told everyone that Sir Wilfrid said that Mavis Pellington was the _____.
4 Then he said that Lady Blemley wanted to invite Mavis to stay because _____.
5 When Major Barfield asked about his lady friend, he _____.
6 When Lady Blemley asked if he would like to go down to the kitchen for his dinner, he _____.
7 He told everyone that Agnes Resker thought the Blemleys _____ and she only came _____.
8 He said that Mrs Cornett repeated this to Bertie van Tahn, and added _____.

4 **A famous writer once said, 'Saki did not like aunts.' Do you agree? Match these sentences with the aunts in the stories. What do they tell us about the aunts?**

1 She sold the chicken.
2 She told her friends that Leonard had changed a vegetable into a bird.
3 She thought that the strange, naked boy was sweet.
4 When she spoke to the children, she always began with 'Don't . . .'

5 **Match the animals with the descriptions. You can check with the glossary after you have finished. Then say which animal you prefer, and why.**

cat, chicken, cow, elephant, ferret, macaw, pig, rabbit, sheep, wolf

1 a long, low, yellow and brown animal
2 a bird that can learn to talk
3 a bird that people keep for its eggs, and also eat
4 a fat, farm animal that people kill and eat
5 an animal that people keep in their homes
6 a big, grey animal with a very long nose
7 a wild animal like a big dog
8 a small animal with long ears, which lives in holes under the ground
9 a farm animal that people keep for milk and also eat
10 a farm animal that people keep for wool and also eat

6 **Do you agree (A) or disagree (D) with these sentences? Explain why.**

1 It is wrong to keep wild animals in boxes or zoos.
2 It is wrong to eat animals.
3 An animal can be a good friend.
4 Cats are more intelligent than other animals.
5 Animals can understand what people say.

7 **Here are some new titles for the stories. Which titles go with which stories? Which titles do you prefer? Why?**

Sredni Vashtar / The Story-Teller / Gabriel-Ernest / Tobermory / The She-Wolf

The Werewolf	Siberian Magic
A Boring Train Journey	The Ferret-God
Uncomfortable Secrets	Bertha and the Wolf
The Boy Who Killed his Aunt	A Clever Joke
The Boy Who Ate Children	Toast for Tea
The Best Child in the World	The Talking Cat
Louisa and the Sugar	Death of a Brave Boy
Mr Appin's Successful Student	

8 **Which story did you prefer? Write a few sentences to explain why.**

ABOUT THE AUTHOR

Saki's real name was Hector Hugh Monro. He was born in Burma in 1870, but after his mother died, he and his sister and brother went to live with his aunts in Devon, in the south-west of England. His two aunts, Aunt Tom and Aunt Augusta, hated each other and were not interested in children. So, like Conradin, Saki learned to dislike aunts and to dream of a world where animals were stronger than people and could punish them for being cruel and stupid.

In 1893 Saki joined the army in Burma, but became ill and returned to the UK to live in London. From 1902 to 1908, he worked as a writer for a newspaper, *The Morning Post*, and lived in Poland, Russia and Paris. He had published his first book in 1899 – a history called *The Rise of the Russian Empire* – and in 1904 his first book of short stories appeared. This was when he took the name 'Saki'; no one knows why he chose it, but it is the name of a gentle South American monkey and perhaps he felt close to this animal.

People have continued to read and enjoy Saki's clever stories for the past hundred years, because they are often cruel and funny at the same time. He wrote only five books of stories (some of them appeared after his death), and two novels. In 1914, at the beginning of the First World War, he joined the army as an ordinary soldier and was shot through the head and killed in 1916.

OXFORD BOOKWORMS LIBRARY

Classics • Crime & Mystery • Factfiles • Fantasy & Horror
Human Interest • Playscripts • Thriller & Adventure
True Stories • World Stories

The OXFORD BOOKWORMS LIBRARY provides enjoyable reading in English, with a wide range of classic and modern fiction, non-fiction, and plays. It includes original and adapted texts in seven carefully graded language stages, which take learners from beginner to advanced level. An overview is given on the next pages.

All Stage 1 titles are available as audio recordings, as well as over eighty other titles from Starter to Stage 6. All Starters and many titles at Stages 1 to 4 are specially recommended for younger learners. Every Bookworm is illustrated, and Starters and Factfiles have full-colour illustrations.

The OXFORD BOOKWORMS LIBRARY also offers extensive support. Each book contains an introduction to the story, notes about the author, a glossary, and activities. Additional resources include tests and worksheets, and answers for these and for the activities in the books. There is advice on running a class library, using audio recordings, and the many ways of using Oxford Bookworms in reading programmes. Resource materials are available on the website <www.oup.com/bookworms>.

The *Oxford Bookworms Collection* is a series for advanced learners. It consists of volumes of short stories by well-known authors, both classic and modern. Texts are not abridged or adapted in any way, but carefully selected to be accessible to the advanced student.

You can find details and a full list of titles in the *Oxford Bookworms Library Catalogue* and *Oxford English Language Teaching Catalogues*, and on the website <www.oup.com/bookworms>.

THE OXFORD BOOKWORMS LIBRARY
GRADING AND SAMPLE EXTRACTS

STARTER • 250 HEADWORDS

present simple – present continuous – imperative –
can/cannot, must – *going to* (future) – simple gerunds …

Her phone is ringing – but where is it?

Sally gets out of bed and looks in her bag. No phone. She looks under the bed. No phone. Then she looks behind the door. There is her phone. Sally picks up her phone and answers it. ***Sally's Phone***

STAGE 1 • 400 HEADWORDS

… past simple – coordination with *and, but, or* –
subordination with *before, after, when, because, so* …

I knew him in Persia. He was a famous builder and I worked with him there. For a time I was his friend, but not for long. When he came to Paris, I came after him – I wanted to watch him. He was a very clever, very dangerous man. ***The Phantom of the Opera***

STAGE 2 • 700 HEADWORDS

… present perfect – *will* (future) – *(don't) have to, must not, could* –
comparison of adjectives – simple *if* clauses – past continuous –
tag questions – *ask/tell* + infinitive …

While I was writing these words in my diary, I decided what to do. I must try to escape. I shall try to get down the wall outside. The window is high above the ground, but I have to try. I shall take some of the gold with me – if I escape, perhaps it will be helpful later. ***Dracula***

STAGE 3 • 1000 HEADWORDS

... should, may – present perfect continuous – *used to* – past perfect –
causative – relative clauses – indirect statements ...

Of course, it was most important that no one should see
Colin, Mary, or Dickon entering the secret garden. So Colin
gave orders to the gardeners that they must all keep away
from that part of the garden in future. *The Secret Garden*

STAGE 4 • 1400 HEADWORDS

... past perfect continuous – passive (simple forms) –
would conditional clauses – indirect questions –
relatives with *where/when* – gerunds after prepositions/phrases ...

I was glad. Now Hyde could not show his face to the world
again. If he did, every honest man in London would be proud
to report him to the police. *Dr Jekyll and Mr Hyde*

STAGE 5 • 1800 HEADWORDS

... future continuous – future perfect –
passive (modals, continuous forms) –
would have conditional clauses – modals + perfect infinitive ...

If he had spoken Estella's name, I would have hit him. I was so
angry with him, and so depressed about my future, that I could
not eat the breakfast. Instead I went straight to the old house.
Great Expectations

STAGE 6 • 2500 HEADWORDS

... passive (infinitives, gerunds) – advanced modal meanings –
clauses of concession, condition

When I stepped up to the piano, I was confident. It was as if I
knew that the prodigy side of me really did exist. And when I
started to play, I was so caught up in how lovely I looked that
I didn't worry how I would sound. *The Joy Luck Club*

Go, Lovely Rose and Other Stories

H. E. BATES

Retold by Rosemary Border

A warm summer night. The moon shines down on the quiet houses and gardens. Everyone is asleep. Everyone except the man in pyjamas and slippers, standing on the wet grass at the end of his garden, watching and waiting . . .

In these three short stories, H. E. Bates presents ordinary people like you and me. But as we get to know them better, we see that their feelings are not at all ordinary. In fact, what happens to them – and in them – is passionate, and even extraordinary. Could this happen to you and me?

The Picture of Dorian Gray

OSCAR WILDE

Retold by Jill Nevile

'When we are happy, we are always good,' says Lord Henry, 'but when we are good, we are not always happy.'

Lord Henry's lazy, clever words lead the young Dorian Gray into a world where it is better to be beautiful than to be good; a world where anything can be forgiven – even murder – if it can make people laugh at a dinner party.